Dear Parent,

This book will have a special place in the heart of every child who has been shunned by a family pet!

Duncan and Dolores are both four years old. He is a cat; she is a little girl who would like the cat to be her friend. Duncan avoids her, and Dolores feels jealous because the cat clearly prefers to be with her sister, Faye. In the end, it is Faye who helps Dolores figure out how to get Duncan to pay attention to her.

As noted in *Horn Book*, a children's book reviewing service: "The cheerful childlike illustrations are remarkably expressive, clearly showing the rapidly alternating feelings of Duncan and the pleasant sisterly relationship of sensible Faye and bouncy Dolores."

We hope you and your child will enjoy this purr-fectly wonderful story.

Sincerely,

Fritz J. Luecke

Fritz J. Luecke
Editorial Director
Weekly Reader Book Club

DUNCAN & DOLORES

BY BARBARA SAMUELS

SIMON & SCHUSTER BOOKS FOR YOUNG READERS

This book is a presentation of Newfield Publications, Inc.
Newfield Publications offers book clubs for children from
preschool through high school. For further information
write to: **Newfield Publications, Inc.,**
4343 Equity Drive, Columbus, Ohio 43228

Published by arrangement with
Simon & Schuster Books for Young Readers,
Simon & Schuster Chioldren's Publishing Division.
Newfield Publications is a federally registered
trademark of Newfield Publications, Inc.
Weekly Reader is a federally registered
trademark of Weekly Reader Corporation.

1996 edition

READING RAINBOW® is a registered trademark of GPN/WNED-TV.

Simon & Schuster Books for Young Readers,
1230 Avenue of the Americas, New York, NY 10020

Library of Congress Cataloging-in-Publication Data:
Samuels, Barbara. Duncan and Dolores. Summary: Dolores learns to curb some
of her more smothering tendencies and wins the affections of her new pet cat, Duncan.
[1. Cats – Fiction] I. Title. PZ7.S1925Du 1986 [E] 85-17119

ISBN 0-02-778210-7

To JUDITH
and AMANDA

One day Faye and Dolores
saw a sign:

NEEDS A HOME
4 YEARS OLD—HIS NAME
IS DUNCAN.

"He's cute," said Dolores, "and he's
just my age. I want a cat like that."

"But animals run away from you, Dolores."
"I want that cat," said Dolores.
"Poor Duncan," sighed Faye.

The Next Day ...

Duncan was delivered in a case.
"Now you are my cat," said Dolores,
"and you will come out and play with me."

Duncan shot out of the case and disappeared under
a cabinet.

"Oh dear, it's starting already," said Faye.

Later That Night...

"Come to bed, Dolores."
"I'm going to sit here till Duncan comes out."
"Just leave some food by the cabinet. He'll
come out when he's ready," said Faye.

"Okay, but I'll leave him this note
so he'll know where I am."

"Oh, brother," said Faye.

Two Days Later...

"I'm so glad you finally came out, Duncan.
Now we can play dress up."

"Cats don't play dress up," said Faye.

"Duncan does. Today I will wear a beautiful
cape and he can wear this lovely hat."

Duncan didn't want to play dress up.

"I understand, Duncan. You would rather
do tricks. I will throw this ball and you
will bring it back to me. *Go get it, Duncan!*"

Duncan didn't want to do tricks.

"Here, Duncan," called Faye softly, "you
don't have to do tricks." Duncan walked
over to Faye and sat in her lap.

The Next Morning...

"Duncan doesn't like me," said Dolores.
"He likes you better than me."

"I think he's afraid of you," said Faye.

"Duncan afraid of me, how silly!"

"You're not afraid of me, are you, Duncan?"

"How come you always play with Faye?"

"You never play with me!"

"It isn't fair!"

"It would be a lot quieter around here if you'd leave that poor cat alone," Faye grumbled.

"That's fine with me," said Dolores. "I have better things to do than chase that fat cat."

Dolores made a hiding place with chairs and an old blanket.

Then she had tea with Martha and Mabel.
She did not ask Duncan to join them.

After tea she played the piano
and refused to notice Duncan.

And when she took her nap she hugged
her teddy bear, not Duncan.

Later That Day...

NOW, LOOK WHAT YOU'VE DONE!

Duncan rolled the paintbrush toward
Dolores. It stopped at her feet.

"Why, thank you, Duncan," said Dolores.
Duncan purred softly.

That Night…

"Duncan sat on my easel today," said Dolores.
"Really," said Faye.

"Then he brought me my paintbrush."
"That's nice," said Faye.

"Look, Faye," whispered Dolores,
"look at Duncan...."

"His chin is on my neck and it tickles....Faye,"

"Uh-oh!"